SUPERTATO

EVILTATO VS. SUPERPEA

Meet Sue and Paul:

Sue Hendra and **Paul Linnet** have been making books together since 2009 when they came up with *Barry the Fish with Fingers*, and since then they haven't stopped. If you've ever wondered which one does the writing and which does the illustrating, wonder no more . . . they both do both!

For lovely Dr. K

SIMON & SCHUSTER

Celebrating 100 Years of Publishing Since 1924

First published in Great Britain in 2024 by Simon & Schuster UK Ltd • 1st Floor, 222 Gray's Inn Road, London, WC1X 8HB

Text and illustrations copyright © 2024 Sue Hendra and Paul Linnet

The right of Sue Hendra and Paul Linnet to be identified as the authors and illustrators of this work has been asserted by them in accordance with the Copyright, Designs and Patents Act, 1988

A CIP catalogue record for this book is available from the British Library upon request

978-1-3985-1170-5 (PB) • 978-1-3985-1171-2 (eBook) • 978-1-3985-1238-2 (eAudio) • Printed in China • 10 9 8 7 6 5 4 3 2 1

SUPERTATO
EVILTATO VS. SUPERPEA

SUE HENDRA
PAUL LINNET

SIMON & SCHUSTER
London New York Sydney Toronto New Delhi

It was night-time in the supermarket and the peas and veggies were enjoying their favourite comic books . . .

"You're SO, SO evil," said the little peas. "We love you, Mean Bean!"

"You're SO, SO good," sighed the veggies. "Hurray for Kindly Kiwi!"

WHAT?!

thought the pea.
But I'm the most evil one,
not some nitwit bean!

OH! thought Supertato.
Maybe I can be **even** better?
And as good and kind as Kindly Kiwi!

But how?!

Luckily, help was at hand.
On the back of the Mean Bean comic book
there was a large advertisement . . .

Excellent, thought the pea,
I'm not going to be 'out-meaned' by a bean!

There was one on the back of the
Kindly Kiwi comic book, too!

WANT TO BE AS
GOOD AS ME?

DON'T DELAY,
SEND AWAY FOR
YOUR KINDLY KIWI
KIND KIT TODAY!

BECOME 400
TIMES MORE KIND
OR YOUR
MONEY BACK!

Oh goodie, thought Supertato,
this is just what I need!

When the parcels arrived,

Evil Pea and Supertato couldn't wait to
see what was inside.

Without delay, both opened their boxes and POOF!

Some sort of sparkly dust filled their faces.

But who had delivered the parcels?
And why were they laughing like that?
Maybe whoever it was knew what
was about to happen.

Something big, something bad,
and very, very . . .

RAH
HA HA
HA HA!

"I'm stuck to the ceiling!"
cried Cucumber.

"Who turned the lights off?"
yelled Tomato.

"Somebody get me out
of here," begged Broccoli.

"It can't be true ..."
whispered Carrot.

"What can't be true?"
called Cucumber from the ceiling.

“Supertato’s gone

BAD!”

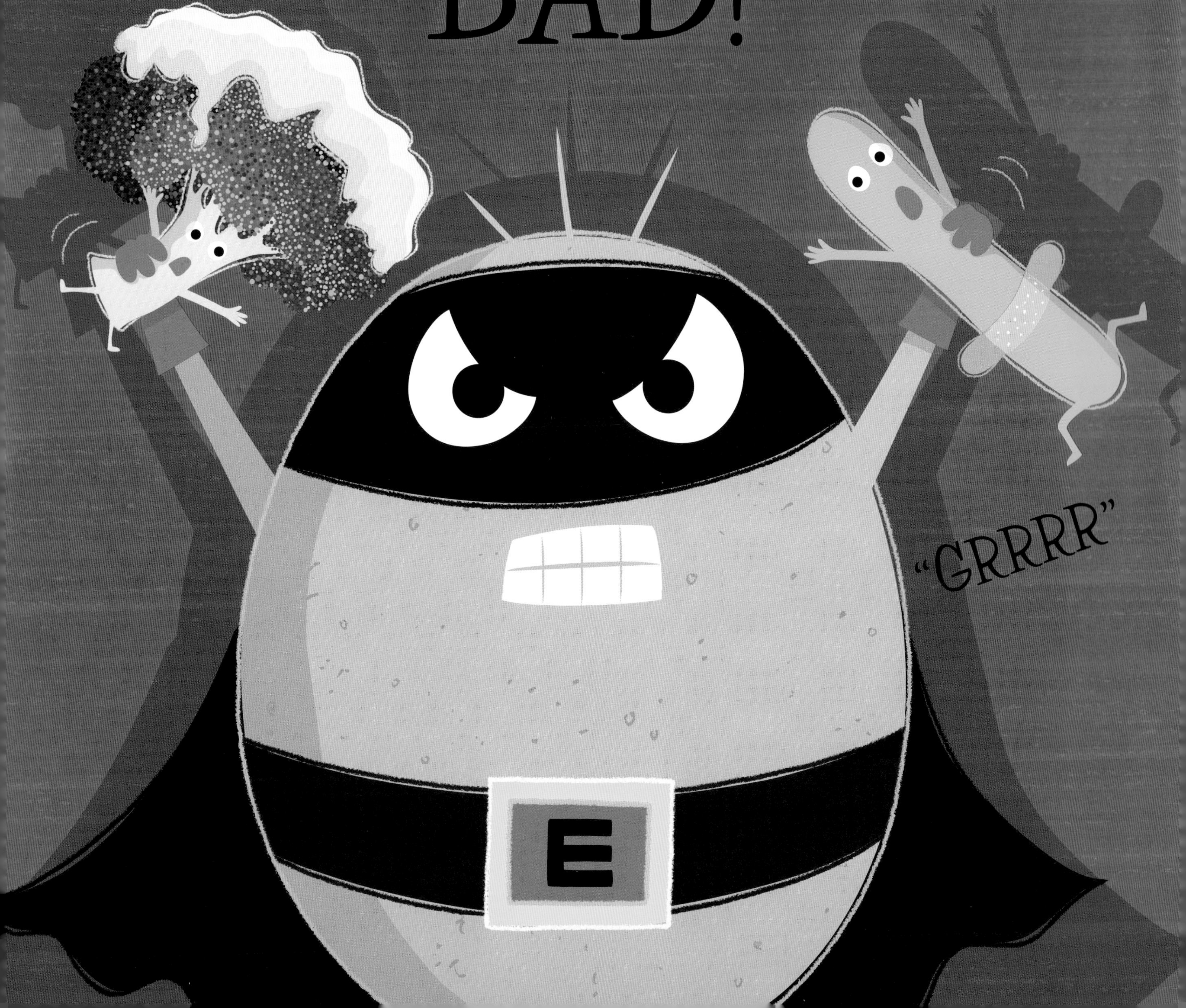

"If that's true," said one pineapple to another, "who's going to save us?"

"Nobody, that's who!" cried Cucumber.

"Let's not be too hasty!" said a cheerful voice.

"Who was that?" asked Broccoli.

Superpea was kind,

Superpea was sweet

and Superpea was thoughtful.
Something was clearly very wrong.

And the wrong kept getting wrong-er because Eviltato was unstoppable.

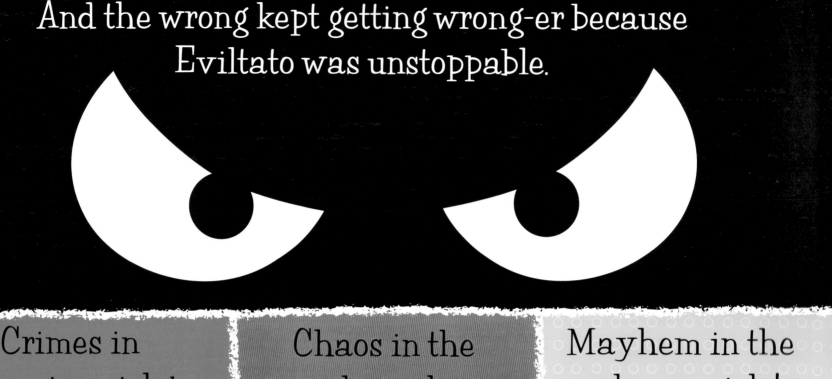

Crimes in the crisp aisle!

Chaos in the cake aisle!

Mayhem in the make-up aisle!

Eviltato was on a rampage!

"Where's he going now?"
said one pineapple
to another.

"Looks to me like he's
going to squirty-cream
the whole supermarket ..."

And they were right.
"We've got to stop this!"
yelled Carrot. "He's out of control!"

"How about I pop the kettle on
and make us a nice cup of tea?"
suggested Superpea.

Luckily, Carrot had found the instructions for the kit hidden inside the box . . .

"It says here that the only way to reverse the evil is with . . .

kindness!"

"Well, that's perfect!" said the pea with glee, "because I'm absolutely full of it!"

And he was!

"Anyone for a sing-song?"

"No thanks, Superpea.
I think I've got an idea," said Carrot,
"but I'm going to need your help."

Everyone gathered round and
Carrot explained the plan.
"Let's do it!"
shouted the veggies.

"I need to know
who's ready!"
yelled the pea . . .

"Veggies on the bottom shelves?"

"Yes, Pea!"

"Veggies on the top shelves?"

"Ready, Pea!"

"Veggie on the ceiling?"

"All set, Pea!"

"Ok, then, 3...2...1...

And once the hugging started, the attack intensified.

"Supertato, we **love** you."

"Supertato, you're the best friend a veggie could have."

"Supertato, you're perfect just the way you are."

Could this be the end of Eviltato?

The veggies held their breath
and crossed their little
veggie fingers.

Then, all of a sudden, as quick as a
flash and without any warning,
Eviltato sprang to life.

He grabbed Cucumber
with one hand,

Superpea with the
other, and . . .

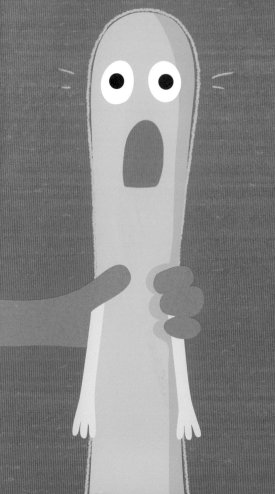

. . . hugged them back.

"Thank you, all of you, you've made me good again."

By this point, the little peas had completely had enough.

One of them handed
Superpea an
ice cream . . .

"FOR ME?!"

. . . and another knocked it
to the floor.

It was an act SO horrible,
SO despicable and mean . . .

. . . that the little peas got just what they wanted.

"Hurray!" they cheered. "The Evil Pea is evil again!"

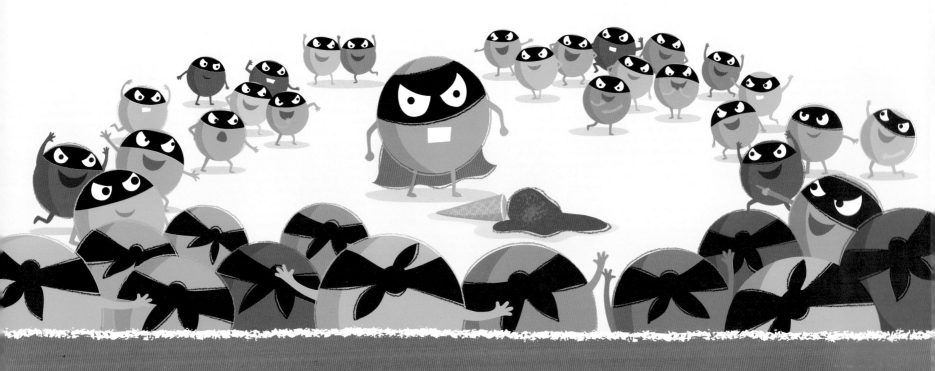

"Mwah ha ha ha ha," shrieked the pea with delight.

Everything in the supermarket
was most certainly back
to normal.

"You know, Supertato, you're **much** better than Kindly Kiwi. For a start, you're **real!**"

"Yes, and **you** are **more** than evil enough for us, Evil Pea!" said the little peas.

"And Mean Bean doesn't actually exist, she's just a made-up character!"